A Silent Vibe…

Dedicated to all the beautiful souls who embark on a quest for their happiness, whose journey transforms them, leading them to realize that their true happiness is not around them but within them.....

A Quest for Happiness…

Fatima Rizvi

Chapter 1

Once upon a time, there was a King whose name was Edward Louis. He became a king at a very early age after the miserable death of his father, King Harrison Louis. Six months after the death of his father, his beloved mother also passed away.

King Edward was twenty-four years old. He was a rational, practical man and a person who always liked victories, He was a prideful King as well.

But as time passed, Edward started feeling sadness. Day by day, he became anxious. He was very tired. Furthermore, he was tired of everything around him. He became cruel & rude to the people of his kingdom.

Life seemed meaningless to him, he questioned himself in his mind

King Edward: what is this happening to me? Why am I not happy?

King Edward: why do I feel exhausted all the time?

Why do I feel like" my heart is burdened" Why do I

feel empty and sad in spite of having everything?

He drew the curtain of his glass window to see the

sun, someone knocked on the door

Courtier: "Your Majesty" King Harold has arrived.

King Edward: Make him sit. I am coming.

The courtier bowed and left the room

King Harold was the king from another kingdom and a

beloved friend of Edward. He came there to get some

help from Edward for war purposes. Edward agreed to

send some soldiers with weapons and horses to help

Harold in the war.

A few days later a horseman came to the palace from

King Harold's side, he gave a letter to one of Edward

courtiers, and the courtier handed it over to King

Edward

Edward read the letter

 My Dear Friend...

Firstly, I am glad to inform you that I defeated our enemy .My kingdom is safe now and there is no more danger here.

I couldn't have done it without you Edward. Without your help, I would not be able to win this battle.

Thank you for your help and support.

Secondly would be happy to let you know that I have organized a royal dinner to celebrate our victory tomorrow night. It would be my pleasure if you could come and joins us.

Harold Williamson...

The next day, Edward went to Harold's palace for a Royal dinner. Kings from different places were invited in the evening. The grand celebration of their victory was held at the palace, the hall was decorated, and King Harold also organized things for their entertainment. Everyone was enjoying dinner.

 After dinner, it was time for the ball

King Harold: Edward, Let me introduce you to Princess Virginia Williamson.

A very beautiful girl in a red gown came downstairs, Harold held her hand and got her to the centre of the hall, and they started dancing, Virginia's presence filled a whole room with happiness and joy.

After a while, Harold introduced her to Edward

King Harold: King Edward...my friend...

King Harold: Virginia is my sister Edward.

Virginia: it's nice to meet you. My brother talks about you a lot.

 King Edward: But I am afraid to say that he never talks about his sister.

Virginia smiled

Princess Virginia: I am wondering if you could dance with me.

 She extended her hand

They started dancing, and Virginia felt an instant attraction to Edward, she was enjoying the ball, but Edward was still not happy but pretending to be

King Edward: Allow me, I have to leave now, Princess.

Princess: it was so nice dancing with you, Thank you for being my ball companion.

King Edward: Pleasure is all mine.

Then Edward came to Harold and asked him to go and then left the place, Virginia smiled even after he had left, and Harold smiled to see her

King Harold: I knew, you would like him.

Princess Virginia: It was the best evening ever. He is exactly the man I dreamed of.

 They smiled

Edward came back to his palace after having this spectacular evening, Edward still felt unhappy, he didn't understand why he felt so unhappy all the time. He couldn't find the reason behind his unhappiness, so he lay on the bed and thought about how happy the people were there at dinner, and then he fell asleep

The next day, Edward left the palace to roam around his kingdom, he always walked around his kingdom to see how things were going there in his kingdom and is everything going according to the system or not.

But this time he had something else in his mind.

To find the reason behind his gloom. To find something that he couldn't find in the palace,

&

Chapter 2

He was walking through the street, there was a Carpenter who was cutting a big wooden plank, and King Edward entered his factory. Carpenter raised his head to see.

Carpenter: OH, My Lord, Accept my greetings

 He bowed and then brought a chair for him .

Carpenter: Have a seat. Joining his hands

Carpenter: "You would have called me if you needed me, Your Majesty" Why did you bother to come yourself?

Edward did not answer

 Carpenter was scared & shocked too why the king himself came to his factory

Carpenter: Has this slave done something wrong, My Lord?

King Edward: Nothing, Nothing like that.

Carpenter: May I ask ... what brings you here in my small factory?

Edward didn't answer first, the carpenter was still standing joining his hands, and his clothes were torn. He was sweating.

King Edward: Answer me one question.

King Edward: Do you love your work?

Carpenter: yes. I... I do sir

King Edward: Are you happy in your life?

Carpenter: yes I am. Nowadays I have many orders by God's grace.

Everyone praises me for my work Your Majesty.

King Edward was looking at him. The carpenter was smiling telling about how his work had been flourishing day by day

King said nothing but left

Carpenter: your Majesty

As King Edward walked away, his mind was clouded with thoughts of the carpenter, He couldn't help but wonder about the happiness the carpenter possessed, despite his torn clothes and sweaty appearance

Edward walked further and entered a sword factory, he stood at the entrance of the sword factory, observing the flurry of activity and the sparks flying from the metalworks, his curiosity piqued, and he stepped forward to get a closer look.

After a while, he went in, there were swords, metals, and unfinished blades scattered all around the workshop.

And in the centre, a boy around eighteen years, was playing with a sword, skilfully twirling it in his hand. His movements were fluid and precise, and Edward couldn't help but admire his dexterity.

Boy: Heeeeee yaaaa. Ah … Ah … ho, not bad Markey.

 He said to himself and turned

Boy: Oops…

Edward saved his head from getting hit by a stray swinging sword, swiftly grabbing it out of the air.

Boy: Pardon me, Pardon me...Majesty. I... I... I didn't see you.

King Edward: You are good at it I must say.

Boy: ohh. OH... No. I mean. I... I was just. I mean ... i am not good at it but... I am good at making it I would say... your majesty.

King Edward: Where did you learn this?

Boy: My father taught me how to make swords. It's him, who is the owner of this factory and I help him to run the factory, Your Majesty.

 Boy was shivering while talking to him

 King Edward: I asked. Where did you learn swordplay? I must admit your swordplay is quite impressive young lad.

Boy: OH... I learned it from one of my cousins Your Majesty. He is a soldier in your army.

King Edward: OH

Boy: yes

King Edward: what about you? Do you too want to join the army? What do you want to be?

Boy: I'd love to do that Your Majesty. But...

King Edward: um- hmmm

Boy: I am the only son my father has. And my Father is one of the best sword smiths in this town. He wants me to run the factory.

King Edward: Anything else you can think of ? A soldier? As you are skilled.

Boy: It's my Father's dream to see me as one of the best blade smiths in the town and run the factory after him. In an efficient way as he does.

He seemed very happy telling this.

 Edward First looked at him and then he left

Boy: your Majesty…… Sir...

 But Edward left

Boy: Did I say something wrong? He said to himself

But that day, Edward noticed something. People of his kingdom were scared of him very much. They don't feel comfortable talking to him He went back to his palace, but his search didn't end.

The next day he woke up, and while having his breakfast he thought of something.

King Edward: I better not wear Royal attire. I should wear something casual. He said to himself

He ordered his commander to bring the tailor into the palace, the tailor was summoned. Tailor took his measurements

King Edward: I want something in which nobody can recognize me.

Tailor: understood your Majesty. Your order will be obeyed.

 He bowed down and left the palace

The next day tailor brought him a dress. A long black trench coat, pants, a black hat, and a mask... it fit well on the King,

Edward appreciated his work and granted him a reward. Tailor became happy, he thanked the king and left the palace.

Edward thought something, something he never thought before... to see the tailor's happy face.

The next day he put on his clothes and left the palace for his search...

This time he walked through the fields. It was a sunny day, and Edward felt hot.

Suddenly he saw the farmers harvesting the crops, He came close to one of them

He was an old man, he was dark, his head was grey, and his beard was also grey.

King Edward: Excuse me, sir.

Old man turned back

Old man: Ohh, hello Gentleman.

King Edward: Hello Sir. I am wondering if you could do me a favour.

Old man: Sure.

King Edward: Actually, I am a Visitor here, in this town.

Old man: oh I see. How can I help you dear?

King Edward: I want to meet the king. Could you please tell me the way to the palace?

 Old man: Sure

The old man told him the address and the way to the palace.

King Edward: Thank you so much, sir.

Old man: No problem

The old man smiled at him

King Edward: it's hot today, isn't it?

Old man: yes it is.

King Edward: Can I ask you something, sir? If... if you don't mind.

Old man: Sure.

King Edward: Do you love work here?

Old man: yes. I do. My crop is like my child. I love taking care of it.

King Edward: would you mind if I ask you something else?

Old man: No problem. Ask me

King Edward: Do you think about any other work instead of farming?

Old man: ha-ha. At this age. No. Not at all. Son... I have given my whole life to this crop. I always believed God had chosen me for this job. And i work hard so that the people of our town don't face any problems regarding food.

King Edward: I am sure you are happy and satisfied in your life.

Old man: No doubt I am. I feel happy to see that everyone has sufficient food to eat here.

 The Old man's face was bright with happiness and full of joy like a shining star.

Edward thought of something

King Edward: Thank you, Sir, for the address... have a nice rest of your day.

Old man: you're welcome my son. You too.

And Edward left the place.

&

Chapter 3

Edward walked further. He felt thirsty. He saw a tree some steps away from him. He went close and sat under the tree.

King Edward: Everyone is happy here. Am I only the person who is not happy in this world? He said to himself

King Edward: why? I have everything in my life. Comfort, Money, Respect, Reputation. Then why?
 He thought

He was thirsty so he walked towards the river. He removed his mask and quenched his thirst. After drinking water from the river.

He saw a woman sitting on the opposite side of the river.

The woman was making a pot, she had a small pottery shop on the other side of the river.

After a while her son came to her, he sat down on the ground and collected some mud in his small hands then started copying her mother. They both laughed. They both were enjoying it. Edward was watching them standing on the other side of the river. He smiled... and he thought.

King Edward: These people have nothing but a small pottery shop. But they are happy. He said to himself

After a while He left from there

 He walked further, He reached the garden where kids were playing with marbles, after a while one marble rolled and hit Edward's feet

Edward picked it up and looked at it. It was a beautiful marble sun rays were falling on it. Edward was still looking at the marble suddenly a boy approached him.

Boy: it's mine. Could you please give it back to me?

Edward looked at him, he was a boy around eight, having big blue eyes, and curly blonde hair. Edward returned it to him and the boy went back to play.

Edward sat down under the tree and looked at those kids. He started watching them play.

They were shouting, playing, fighting but enjoying.

They were enjoying themselves and were happy.

Edward didn't realize he was smiling watching their actions. Edward had never seen playing kids before.

He thought "Had he ever played games in his childhood?

The answer was "No"

Since his childhood, Edward was taught how to behave like a king. How do Kings rule the Kingdom? His entire childhood and teenage had been spent in wars. Edward was thinking all this when he heard a voice

"Bye ...

The match was over now, Kids started going back to their homes.

Within no time, the garden became empty,

Edward noticed something, one kid didn't go to his home. He was still sitting on the ground and counting his marbles.

Edward came to him. The boy looked at him.

It was the same boy whose marble had hit Edward's feet.

King Edward: Are you not going back?

 Edward asked him

Boy: No..

 He replied

King Edward: why?

Boy: why would I tell you?

King Edward: Sorry.

Boy: Are you a Kidnapper?

King Edward: No... I am not.

Boy: who are you then?

King Edward: I am a visitor here. Edward replied

Boy: You are lying. I saw you watching us play.

King Edward: yes, I admit I was watching.

Boy: Proved... You lied....

King Edward: About what?

Boy: That you are not a kidnapper. Look if you are. I tell you, I am not scared of you. You understand that.

King Edward: I am not a kidnapper as I told you before.

 He continued

King Edward: I have come here to explore this place.

 Boy: okay then.

King Edward: yes.

King Edward: May I know your name?

Boy: Michael.

King Edward: So Michael. You aren't scared of kidnappers... huh?

He sat down on the ground next to Michael

Michael: yes...I am not. I am not scared of anyone. If I found one of them, I would throw my marble at his eyes and would hit him hard.

King Edward: Ohh. Brave boy

Michael: yes. Lily says "We should not scared of anyone.

King Edward: And who is Lily?

Michael: OH... Lily is my elder sister.

King Edward: okay.

Michael: you didn't tell me your name by the way.

King Edward: My name is Edward.

Michael: Edward..Ohh..

King Edward: What happened?

Michael: just.. I didn't like your name.

King Edward: what?

Michael: I just hate this name.

King Edward: Why? Why is that?

Michael: Come here, bring your ear closer.

Edward leaned in and the boy whispered in his ear

Michael: Our king has the same name. He is a bad King. If I were a king, I would be a good King.

He continued

Michael: He doesn't love the people of his kingdom. He doesn't care about us. He is cruel. Lily says, she also doesn't like him. But please... Edward... Don't tell anyone. Otherwise, my sister and I will be in trouble.

Edward got silent after listening to the words of little boy

Michael: Promise me you won't tell anyone.

Michael extended his little finger to make a promise

Michael: Promise?

King Edward: I promise.

Edward too extended his finger to make a promise

Michael: you seem a good man, we can be friends.

Edward stood up from the ground and started thinking something

Michael: what happened?

King Edward: Nothing. Yes, we can be friends.

Michael smiled at him, so Edward did

Michael: OH. It's going to be sunset. Lily would be back home soon. I must leave.

Michael: I have to go Edward.

Michael: Bye.

King Edward: Bye.

Michael stopped and turned to him

Michael: Edward, will you come here tomorrow?

King Edward: I don't know.

Michael: OH. It's okay. Take care of yourself. Bye

King Edward: you too.

And Michael went away from there

&

Chapter 4

Edward went to his palace

King Edward: Am I really cruel? I haven't realized people in my Kingdom are not happy with me. He thought

Days passed, One day Edward ordered his commander to organize a fair in the town. The commander followed the order and made an announcement in the state.

Commander: "May I have your attention, please?

"Our beloved King has ordered to organize a fair in the kingdom tomorrow evening. All the people of the state are invited"

People were very happy to hear that

The next evening, the fair was organized right in front of the palace. The place was decorated with lights. Different kinds of stalls were there at the fair. Games stalls for fun, food stalls, craft stalls, Toy stalls, garments stalls, jewellery stalls for women. All were free.

People could take whatever they wanted to. People were very happy and enjoying there. Kids were taking rides... some kids were playing with toys. Some had their hands full of different toys like camel, lion, and elephant.

Some kids were standing near the stage to see the clown show. Some had cotton candy in their hands. They were excited.

Some people were enjoying their food. Women were trying jewellery on them.

All the people were happy and having fun.

Edward was watching them through the window of his palace. He smiled to see their happy faces and the joyful environment around his palace.

That moment he felt something. Something which was giving him pleasure. That day "He felt happy"

Suddenly someone knocked on his door, it was commander.

Commander: 'Your Majesty.. King Harold has come downstairs.

 King Edward: King Harold?

Commander: yes. I wonder if you have invited him to join the fair.

King Edward: I don't remember i did... Well... send him up

 Commander bowed then left the room

Edward put on his royal mantle, King Harold came up.

King Harold: Oh my dear, you are there.

Harold hugged him

King Edward: How are you? It's so nice to see you here.

King Harold: I am fine. What's going on here outside of the palace?

King Edward: Nothing special. Just trying to do something...

King Harold: something?

King Edward: something good... for the people.

King Harold: Listening to that made me happy.

King Edward: And I realized something. A moment ago.

King Harold: what is that?

King Edward: When you do something for others, which makes them happy. It feels good. You also feel happy inside.

King Harold: Seems, I have come at the right time.

King Edward: What does that mean?

King Harold: Edward, I want to talk to you about something.

King Edward: please have a seat.

 Pointed at his bed

They both sat down on the bed and Harold started talking about the purpose behind his arrival.

King Harold: Edward, as you know you are my best friend and I know you are the great king as well. You are brave, strong, and a loyal friend.

Someone knocked on the door

Commander: May we come in Your Majesty?

The Commander came with a servant who brought a trolley on which a pot was kept with two glasses. After serving drinks to Edward and Harold. Commander gestured for the servant to go. Harold looked at the commander.

Commander: Excuse me.

He also left

Harold continued.

King Harold: Edward, I have come here to give you a proposal.

King Edward: A proposal?

King Harold: I want to see my sister happily married to you. I want you to get married to her. My Friend.

King Edward: OH...you must excuse me my friend...

King Harold: Edward, it's my desire.

King Edward: Harold... I understand. But... I have never thought about being tied up with anyone. I have never thought about marriage.

King Harold: Not an issue. You can think about it now.

King Edward: No. No... You didn't understand.

King Harold: what's wrong with Virginia?

King Edward: No, you are taking me wrong, it's not Virginia. She is perfect. She is a brilliant, vibrant & beautiful girl, I must say.

King Harold: so what? What is the problem then?

King Edward: Harold. I... I don't know.

King Harold: Do you have feelings for someone else?

King Edward: No... I have never thought of getting married. I have never felt for anyone. Harold got upset

King Edward: Your sister can find someone far better than me, Harold.

King Harold: I recon she has feelings for you.

King Edward: How could that be? I only met her once.

King Harold: There is no condition for falling in love...That you need to meet thousands of times to be in love with someone. It just happens, when it's meant to happen Edward.

King Edward: Harold. You must excuse me my friend but I don't believe in that.

King Harold: Allow me Edward. I should leave now.

King Edward: No, please. You haven't had dinner.

King Harold: No Edward...I am not feeling hungry at the moment. Take care.

 King Harold left

King Edward: Harold...

He whispered

Chapter 5

The next day Edward wore his casual outfit and started walking across town, he was roaming around the streets of the kingdom. People were happy they were talking about the last evening they had spent at the fair.

They were showing things they brought from the fair.

Edward smiled to see them happy then walked further.

He saw Michael, who was showing a slingshot to his friends which he brought from the fair.

Kids were very happy, happy vibes were all around the town. Some showed toy guns, some had dolls in their hands.

As Edward walked further someone called his name "Edward"

Michael: Edward. Stop

Edward turned around and looked at Michael

King Edward: OH. You there. How are you, little boy?

Michael: I am so Happy Today. Look what I've got from the fair. My slingshot... isn't it cool?

King Edward: yes it is.

They were talking on their way

Michael: I've brought so many toys. Even Lily took four dresses for her. Because it was free of cost Edward. Lily had only three frocks, she had been wearing them for a very long time.

King Edward: OH

They were crossing the garden now

Michael: yes. She had only three. Because she bought me some new clothes a few months ago, that's why she couldn't afford for herself.

King Edward: OH.

Michael: Actually, we are very poor & she doesn't earn enough. That's why... But now I am happy for her. Now she has something new to wear. I got bored seeing her in those dresses.

And you know what, I also picked some hairclips for her and put them in my pocket and I surprised Lily...

Lily didn't know about my stealing.

Michael laughed

King Edward: but I heard, everything was free there, how would that be stealing?

Michael: No. It was stealing. Lily says 'when we pick someone's thing without permission, we steal that"

And I did the same. The Stall owner didn't know that I picked up those hairclips. He was doing something else when I hid those clips in my pocket.

Michael put a hand on his mouth and looked at Edward, Edward laughed and ruffled his hair

Michael: You tell me, what did... you bring from the fair?

King Edward: I... I...

Edward started thinking

Michael: Ohho Edward... You didn't bring anything. Why? It was free. Do you know what free means?

You didn't need to pay. Why didn't you bring anything for you?

"Well, you look, Rich. I think...you don't need anything.

Edward was silent, Michael questioned him and he answered it himself, Edward was enjoying seeing Michael

Michael: okay. You took rides, did you?

King Edward: No.

Michael: Edward, Did you go to the fair?

King Edward: No. I thought maybe only the townspeople were invited. I am a stranger here... that's why.

Michael: Ohh. I see.

King Edward: yeah.

Michael: I am home now. It's there. Pointed the hut behind the trees

King Edward: OH.

Michael: would you like to come?

King Edward: Not now. I have some work to do.

Michael: okay... Bbye

King Edward: bye

Edward smiled at him, and the boy went to his home.

It was a very small dilapidated hut where Michael lived.

 Edward saw Michael until he went into the hut.

ॐ

Chapter 6

Days passed...

Edward often used to meet Michael on his way. Sometimes Edward would come into the garden to see the kids, whenever Edward appeared in the garden Michael stopped playing with the kids and came to him, sat down under the tree, next to him and started talking to him.

Edward also was enjoying his company. He took great interest in Michael's talks. Edward noticed his innocent expressions while Michael spoke.

They became friends. Michael also got attached to him. Edward hadn't realized but he was transforming. And he started living happily again. He started paying more attention to the people of his kingdom.

Everyone in the kingdom started liking him.

Edward would make new strategies for the good of the kingdom. He used to hear the problems of the people and would try to solve them.

He also introduced some new laws in the kingdom.

One day Edward ordered his commander

King Edward: Commander, food grains to be delivered to every single house in the town. And make sure nobody would go to bed on an empty stomach.

Commander obeyed his order.

It had been a week. Edward didn't come to the garden, and Michael was upset.

One day Michael came back to his home from the garden, and he looked sad.

Lily: Michael. Welcome back

 Michael didn't answer

Lily: What happened to my little brother? Is he going to tell me?

 Michael: I am sad.

Lily: Aww... Why is that?

Michael: Edward, I am worried about him.

Lily: Edward?

Michael: He is my friend. I once told you about him, I thought him a Kidnapper. Do you remember?

Lily: yeah ... I remember. I forbade you to talk to that stranger.

Michael: But... He is Nice & Now he is my friend.

Lily: Ohh...

Lily: So, why are you worried... what's wrong with him... Is he okay?

Michael: I don't know where he is. It's been a week since I haven't met him.

Lily: Maybe he is busy.

Michael: But he always comes.

Lily: Maybe he has gone, as you told me he was a visitor here.

Michael: Gone?

Michael's heart just smashed tears started falling down from his eyes

Lily: I don't know... Look, Michael, stop crying... I was just guessing ... maybe... maybe he is here.

Lily: Stop crying Michael... let's have dinner. Come

 Michael: I don't feel like eating anything.

Lily: please.

Michael: No. Michael cried

Lily: He will come tomorrow, surely.

 Michael: How do you know that?

Lily: Uhhh... I am telling you. He will come.

Michael: But...

Lily: You will see, but you have to wait till tomorrow for that. And for now, come. Eat something.

The next day Michael was sitting, waiting under the tree, the wind was blowing, an Hour passed, and he was tired of waiting. He stood up to go but he heard his name behind.

King Edward: Michael. Hey... stop...

Michael turned back

Michael: Edward...

Michael was very happy to see him

Michael: Where have you been Edward?

King Edward: I was out of the town.

Michael: I thought you were gone. Gone forever.

King Edward: Gone?

Michael: Because you are a visitor to our town. You told me that,

King Edward: oh yeah... but now. I am thinking of staying here forever.

Michael: Really?

King Edward: um-hmm

Edward smiled at him

Michael: whoa-ho... Edward is not going. He will stay here... forever. Wuhu Michael was happy to hear that. And he started dancing

Michael: I am so happy Edward.

King Edward: So am I.

Michael: You know what Edward, when I was worried about you yesterday...

King Edward: You were worried about me?

Michael: yes, I was. Let me complete it first.

King Edward: Oh Sorry. Accept my apology.

Michael: ha-ha. Apology accepted.

They both laughed

Michael: Where was I?

He thought

King Edward: You were saying something like, "You were worried about me"

Michael: Oh yeah. When I was worried about you yesterday, Lily told me that you would come today. & see. You came.

Michael: I wonder, Lily knows everything. Isn't she Awesome?

King Edward: She is, no doubt.

King Edward was smiling, Michael looked at him & smiled strangely as he was thinking something. Edward noticed his gaze

King Edward: What?

He asked

Michael: You are handsome.

King Edward: OH…. Well… Thank you.

Michael: You are tall, brave, and charming.

 King Edward: um-hmm.

Michael: If you were like us, I would give my sister's hand in yours. You would be a perfect man for her.

King Edward: Like you?

Michael: Poor. We are very poor, Edward.

Edward didn't say anything but listen to his innocent talks

Michael: Lily once told me, we were rich too. When we had our parents. Our Father was a merchant. I was three when they died. Lily was sixteen.

King Edward: How did they die?

Michael: I don't know, Lily never told me that.

King Edward: Oh I am sorry.

Michael: Why are you saying Sorry, you didn't kill my parents.

Edward looked at Michael, Michael's facial expressions were describing his innocence and kind heart and his pure soul.

Michael: I am finding a perfect match for Lily. I am worried about her. She is twenty one now. I am so worried.

King Edward: You are...worried?

Michael: Yes, of course, I am her brother. It is my responsibility, isn't it?

 King Edward: Hahaha.

Michael: What are you laughing at? Isn't it my responsibility?

King Edward: yes, of course...of course...it is.

Michael: Lily performs all her duties very well. She works hard to provide for me. What am I doing for my sister...? Nothing.

Michael: I am not a good brother, I think.

King Edward: No... You are.

Michael: No. I am a bad brother.

 Michael screamed

 Michael: "OH JESUS"

King Edward: What happened?

Michael: I forgot, Lily asked me to buy some curd from the market. I have to go. Michael stood up and fled

Michael: I told you that I am not a good brother, now see.

And Michael ran away after saying this .

Edward was smiling

&

Chapter 7

Now, Edward forgot about his search, now, he loved to do his duties. He started living happily. He used to meet everyone pleasantly,

This young boy had impacted his life so much.

He learned, that happiness is nowhere but inside us. We don't need to find it here and there.

Now, everyone loved him, He was the beloved King of his kingdom. King Edward... But for his little friend Michael, he was still Edward. A visitor...

One day Michael & Lily were at the grocery store, there was a toy shop next to the store. Michael saw a toy sword.

Michael: Lily, Can you buy me this?

He pointed the sword

Lily: What?

Michael: This sword.

Lily: Sure, How much for this ?

Lily asked the shopkeeper

Seller: 500 Drachma.

She checked her purse

Lily: Ohhh... Michael, I'll buy you this some other day. She whispered in his ear

Michael: But...

Lily: I promise.

Lily: Now come.

Lily: Thank you, Sir.

She thanked the shopkeeper and turned back but Michael was still standing at the shop & looking at the sword.

Meanwhile, a man came and stood next to Michael.

King Edward: How much, you said?

Shopkeeper: 500 Drachma, Sir.

Michael: Edward?

He screamed

Michael: OH Edward.

Michael was happy to see him

Lily turned back

Shopkeeper: Here you go, Sir.

King Edward: Thank you.

Edward gave a sword to Michael, and Michael got happy after getting it.

 After watching all this. Lily came there

Michael: Lily, "It's him...Edward" My friend.. You remember lily ? & Edward it's my sister Lily...

Lily was a very beautiful girl, pretty like a nymph. Her eyes were fine blue like sparkling sapphire, captivating, holding a secret of the universe. That anyone could lost in them forever as Edward got lost for a second. Her curly blonde hair was like a cascade of silk, as mesmerizing as a gentle breeze. He couldn't help but be enchanted by her beauty looking at her.

At the same time, Lily also felt an instant infatuation with Edward's enigmatic personality.

For a few seconds, time stood still for both of them.

But Lily controlled herself and looked away.

King Edward: Hello...Miss.

Lily: Give it back to him Michael.

 Michael: No.

Lily took the sword from Michael's hand and gave it to Edward

Lily: pardon me, Sir, but we can't take it. She said to Edward

King Edward: But. Why?

King Edward: I am sorry, I should have asked you. But... look. Keep it. As a gift for him.

Michael: It's my gift. Did you hear that Lily?

King Edward: Please.

Lily: When I get my salary, I will pay you for this toy. She said it to Edward

King Edward: No need to pay. Consider it as my gift to him. Please. He smiled to see Michael

Michael: Thank you. Thank you so much, Edward.

 Michael smiled at him too

Lily: Thank you.

King Edward: You are most welcome.

Lily: We have to leave, Michael.

She said to Michael and held his hand

Michael: Bye Edward.

And they left

Edward came back to his palace, and he noticed, he was feeling different. He was thinking about his meeting with Lily.

He tried to suppress those feelings. But he didn't succeed in doing that. Lily's face kept appearing in this thought again and again.

One day Edward went to the wilderness for hunting. He was running after the deer, but the deer disappeared somewhere in the forest. He was looking for it when suddenly his eyes caught two girls across the river.

One of them moved to the right & other started following her path straight. Edward followed her. The girl listened to the footsteps approaching her, she stopped and looked back.

Lily: You?

King Edward: Hello, Miss. Lily. How are you doing?

Lily: Good.

King Edward: I came here for hunting then I saw you.

Lily: Oh.

King Edward: How is Michael?

Lily: He is fine.

King Edward: Nice

Lily: yes. It was nice to meet you, sir.

King Edward: Could I give you company to home? If you... Don't mind.

Lily: It's very nice of you sir, but I don't need it. Thank you.

She left after saying this, Edward got upset initially then he started looking for deer again.

Whenever Edward and Michael used to meet, Edward always wanted to hear about Lily. Edward wanted to know Lily more.

He started going for hunting daily so that he could

see Lily on his way.

51

Chapter 8

One day Edward didn't find Lily, so he went to the place, where their hut was.

He was standing behind the tree and wondering if everything was fine with Michael and Lily.

Straight away, Lily appeared. She carried a bucket in her hand in which wet clothes were. And she had hung the wet clothes on the rope that was tied between two trees.

When she wanted to go back to her hut, she turned back, Edward hid himself behind the tree. But Lily had seen him.

When Edward came back to his palace. He decided to tell Lily about his feelings.

The next day, When Lily was returning from work, Edward started following her, she turned back when she heard footsteps.

Lily: Stop following me Mister.

King Edward: I want to talk to you, Maiden.

Lily: But I don't want to talk to you. I apologise sir

king Edward: Please.

Lily: Okay.

Edward got silent

Lily: Tell me what do you want to talk about?

King Edward: I have been following you for a very long time Miss.

Lily: I know that. You are making me feel uncomfortable.

King Edward: I apologize for that. Miss. I know. It's out of the ordinary, it's not something I usually experience. But I... I feel for you... So.. so deeply.

First Time Edward was not feeling confident

Lily: Pardon me. I have to leave Sir.

King Edward: What happened?

Lily did not answer but taking her steps fast

King Edward: stop. Please ...tell me

Lily: I don't believe you.

King Edward: Believe me.

Lily: Stop stalking me, what do you think of me? "A fool" ... I don't know your Intentions.

King Edward: What?

Lily: yes.

King Edward: I didn't understand.

Lily: Tell me, how could a person who is Rich, well-educated, and so charming, like me? I am poor but not stupid. You must have bad intentions and I know that. So just stay away from me... & yeah my brother as well.

 She ran from the place

King Edward: Stop... Listen to me.

When Lily came to her home, she locked the door. Her heart was pounding.

Michael came to her.

Michael: Lily. What happened? Are you okay? Lily: Nothing.

Michael: No. You are lying. You look worried. Lily: Nothing. I got scolded by my owner today. Michael: Ohhh... What did you do?

Lily: I broke a plate when I was washing dishes. It slipped off my hand. It was an accident.

 Michael: It was not your fault.

Lily: I know that dear.

Michael: Your owner is harsh to you.

Lily: Come here,

She hugged him

Lily: Don't think too much.

 She kissed him

Lily: love you, Michael

She whispered

Michael: I love you too Lily.

One day when Lily and Michael were going to have dinner.

Lily: Michael, I have cooked your favourite soup today.

 Michael: Oh wow. Corn soup.

He got happy

Lily: yes

They were having their soup

Michael: You know what Lily, Edward bought me a corn few days ago when we were in the garden.

Lily: Do you meet him?

Michael: yes. But I didn't meet him today. We met Yesterday.

Lily: Stop meeting him, Michael.

Michael: Why? He is my friend.

Lily: How could he be your friend? He is not even your age.

Michael: He... is my friend. And why would I stop meeting him?

Lily: He is a bad man.

Michael: No. He is not. He is not a kidnapper.

Lily: Michael, Don't meet him again.

Michael: But why? He is a nice man. I know him.

Lily: No. You don't know him.

Michael: But.

Lily: Do you love your sister?

 Michael: yes. I do.

Lily: So stop meeting him.

 Michael: But...

Lily: Promise me,

 Lily: Promise?

 Michael: Okay

Lily had not been going to her work for three days, she thought Edward would meet on her way.

On the other side, Edward failed to get the thought of Lily out of his mind, he called his commander Thomas.

Commander Thomas was a fifty nine year-old man, and he was faithful and loyal to him. He had been serving for the kingdom since Edward's father was alive.

Edward sometimes would take suggestions from him, he was like his father

 The Commander came to him

King Edward: I want to talk to you, Commander Thomas.

Commander: Yes. Please…"Your Majesty.

King Edward: Alone.

And in the next second the hall became empty

Commander: Is everything alright? "Your Majesty"

King Majesty: Yes. I wanted to talk to you about something personal today.

Commander: I see

King Edward: I want your suggestion regarding something.

Commander: Sure. And I will be grateful to guide you to the right path.

King Edward: Thank you commander.

Commander: What is that? Majesty

 For a while, Edward got silent

Commander: I am wondering, for the first time in your whole life I am seeing you thinking so much before telling something.

Commander: It seems...something is disturbing you. "Your Majesty"

King Edward: Commander Thomas. Tell me, what to look for in a person to marry?

Commander: I am glad you asked me for that question.

Commander: As a person or as a king sir?

King Edward: What does that mean?

Commander: I don't want you to get confused "My Lord" But As a king...

King Edward: umm-hmm.

Commander: You must marry...

Commander: A girl, who would help you in handling this whole kingdom, Who knows How to deal with the people of the kingdom, Who should be the Royal Family ,Who is skilled, and learned.

He continued

You should marry a princess. "Your Majesty"

King Edward: A princess?

Commander: yes. Why don't you marry Princess Virginia Williamson, King Harold's sister?

 Edward looked at him

Commander: Pardon me, Your Majesty but my son told me about King Harold's Arrival.

King Edward: No. You are like my father Commander Thomas. Well, I am not ready for marriage at the moment.

Commander: So Why did you ask such a question?

Edward didn't answer and stood up

King Edward: Thank you, Commander Thomas.

Commander: It's my pleasure, Your Majesty.

Commander left the hall

෮

Chapter 9

One day in the evening, Michael was sitting on the stairs out of his house.

Lily came to Michael. Michael looked at the toy sword in his hands which Edward bought him. He looked very sad.

Lily: Michael, come... Let's sleep.

Michael: I haven't met him for four days. Edward must have come to meet me in the garden.

 Lily: Why don't you play with the boys of your age?

Michael: He is my friend and I love him.

He was upset. Lily wanted to make him happy, she held his hand and took him into the hut. She laid him down on the bed, covered him with a blanket & held his hand then sat beside him.

Lily: I tell you one story today.

Michael: okay.

Lily: It's a very good story, you would love it. And Lily started telling him the story

Lily: "A long time ago, there was a King" Since when he was born, it was predicted that.... Michael: wait.

 Michael interrupted her

Lily: What happened dear?

Michael: What was the name of the King?

Lily: Name? Um.

She started thinking... as she wanted to tell his name... Michael said

Michael: Let's assume his name was Edward.

Lily understood that Michael got attached to Edward & he loved him so much. She continued her story and after listening to her story Michael fell asleep

Lily: Good night Dear.

 She kissed him and whispered

She came to the window, it was the only window in their hut. She looked at the sky. The moon and stars.

Lily: OH Mom, Dad, why did you leave us alone? "I am tired" She cried

Lily: Oh GOD "Please. Please help me"

As she wanted to draw the curtain of the window, she saw something out there. She saw a shadow of someone sitting on the horse. It was very dark outside so she couldn't see clearly, who it was. She closed the window and locked the door

The next day when Lily was at work.

Michael came to the garden and sat under the tree, Kids were playing he was watching them.

After a while; Edward came there.

King Edward: Why aren't you playing with them?

Michael: Ohh Edward.

Michael was happy to see him but after a second, he remembered his sister's promise. And he turned his face to the other side

King Edward: What happened? I came here yesterday, but you weren't here.

 He sat down next to him under the tree

 Michael didn't answer

King Edward: Michael?

King Edward: What happened? Is everything okay?

He didn't answer

King Edward: Tell me what is bothering you, little boy.

Michael: Go. Go away.

King Edward: Hey... Michael. What happened to you?

Michael: I don't want to talk to you.

King Edward: Why?

Michael: Because I can't talk to you.

King Edward: What? What are you talking about me? I don't understand.

Michael: I made a promise to Lily not to talk to you.

King Edward: Why? Why is that? Why did you make such a Promise?

Michael: She said "You are a bad man"

King Edward: What?

Michael: Just go from here. Go Please.

Michael cried

King Edward: Michael.

Michael: just go.

King Edward: Okay. Okay... I am leaving.

He whispered

King Edward: Take care.

he left

Michael: Oh Edward I am sorry.

Michael cried more as he watched him go.

One day Edward was going to the forest, and King Harold saw him there. And started following him.

King Harold: Edward. Stop...

Edward stopped his horse and turned back

King Edward: Harold. How do you do? What are you doing here?

King Harold: I came here to meet you in the palace. But when I saw your horse going into the forest, I started following you.

King Edward: Oh I see. I am wondering if you are not angry at me anymore.

King Harold: No... No. I want to apologize for being rude to you that day.

 King Edward: No.

King Harold: Actually... a few days ago I realized, I was pressuring you to get married to Virginia. I was thinking about my sister, but at the same time I forgot about my childhood friend, it's your choice whether you want to marry or not. And of course, it's your choice to choose your companion for your life. I became selfish that day. I shouldn't have been. Please accept my apology.

King Edward: No... Please. Don't be sorry.

King Harold: Thank you Edward. And yeah. I have good news to give you... Virginia has engaged to Prince Phillips.

Prince Phillips proposed to her when she and I went to Egypt after getting invited by King Albert to his daughter's wedding. Virginia accepted his proposal.

King Edward: Nice. I am glad to hear that. I am happy for her.

King Harold: So am I.

They smiled

King Harold looked at the forest, thought something
then smiled.

King Edward: What is that you are thinking about?

King Harold: I am wondering, who will win this time?

 King Edward: In what?

King Harold: In Horse race.

Harold smiled and started riding his horse

King Harold: You will lose this time my friend ha-ha.

King Edward: Let's see.

Edward also rode his Horse, His hat fell off in the air.

King Edward: My hat.

King Harold: I didn't understand the purpose behind
this magician's outfit Edward.

They were riding and talking

King Edward: I will tell you but after the win. Ha-ha

Edward rode his horse so fast that in the next 30
seconds, his horse was out of Harold's sight. He was
enjoying his ride, his long brown hair was flying in
the air

Now, Edward's Horse was far ahead of Harold's horse

He crossed the mountains, river, and trees then he stopped his horse some steps away after seeing Lily and Suzan. They were collecting some apples from the tree and putting them into the basket.

Edward got angry to see her. Lily's gaze fell upon him

Lily: Let's go from here, Suzan.

And they went away

Edward continued his race to the palace and saw that Harold was already there.

King Harold: You lost, "My friend"

King Edward: Indeed...

He smiled at Harold, held his hand, and took him to the palace

৯

Chapter 10

The next day, Lily went to buy shoes for her, her old shoes were worn out.

When she was leaving the store, her eyes fell on Edward, who was giving bread to an old poor man.

The old man thanked him politely, and Edward smiled at him.

As Edward stood up and turned back, he found Lily standing at the door of the shop.

As soon as Lily saw Edward staring at her, she started running fast. Edward followed her.

King Edward: Stop. I said "Stop"

Lily: Stop following me.

King Edward: I want to talk to you.

 She stopped

Lily: What do you want? Why don't you leave me alone?

King Edward: Excuse me. You must have mistaken me, I haven't come here for you. Neither do I wish to get myself insulted again. Answer me one question... What did you say to Michael about me?

Lily got silent and looked away

King Edward: Tell me.

King Edward: Why did you say the wrong things about me to that poor little boy?

Edward was angry

King Edward: Answer me.

Lily: So that he stays away from you. I don't know what you have done to my brother.

King Edward: I liked you, and I know I made a mistake. A big mistake. Because you didn't even consider it necessary to listen to me once. But... don't you dare to bring him into all this.

Lily: He is my brother, I know what is good for him.

She took out something from her purse and put it on Edward's hand

Lily: Take your 500 Drachma and Leave us alone. Please.

 Lily: Have a good day. Goodbye, Sir.

She left

The next day when Lily and Suzan were returning from work

Lily: What do I do?

She told Suzan about Edward

Suzan: Don't you like him?

Lily: I liked him initially, but when I saw his true face...

Suzan: True face? What does that mean?

Lily: Yes. You tell me how that kind of man could like me.

Suzan: I didn't understand.

Lily: He is handsome, isn't he?

Suzan: Indeed, he is.

Lily: He is well-mannered, and educated. He is just like a Prince from a book. Any girl can fall for him easily and would want to marry him. Think to yourself, how can a person like him fall in love with a girl like me? He is lying. He doesn't like me.

Suzan: You mean….

Lily: Yes, exactly. He is not a good man, you don't know him, wherever I go, he follows me, He is a creepy stalker. I am scared. A few days ago I saw him standing in front of my hut, in the evening,

Suzan: Oh Jesus...

Lily: He is dangerous, I am afraid he is a kidnapper.

Suzan: He is not a kidnapper Lily. If he was, he would have kidnapped Michael by now.

 Lily: But Michael. He loves him so much. I am afraid he might turn Michael against me. She cried

Suzan: Stop crying, Lily.

Lily: But what if he takes Michael away from me, what if he is an imposter who first pretends to be a good man then later he takes poor children away with him?

Suzan: No. It won't happen. Lily. Stop crying... Oh, dear.

Suzan: Lily. Listen to me, look at me, Lily.

Suzan wiped her tears

Suzan: I have an idea.

Lily: Idea?

Suzan: You better write a letter to the King.

Lily: King?

Suzan: Yes. Write him a letter about all this.

Suzan: You know, once a lady, who used to live with her only daughter. Someone also would stalk her daughter , so she decided to write a letter to the King.

Lily. What happened then?

Suzan: King Edward took strict action against him. He ordered his commander to find him, then they arrested him.

Suzan: Complaint box is especially for those who are helpless or can't express themselves openly before the King.

Suzan: Yes. You do that. Write it down and then put it in a royal complaint box and wait...

You will be answered. He will take action against this man. Our King is Nice and helpful. He will help you. I am sure.

Lily: Thank you. Thank you so much.

Suzan: Lily. The complaint box is checked every three days. You better send a letter tomorrow so that your turn will come soon.

Lily: Okay.

ॐ

Chapter 11

After listening to the problems of the people in the Royal meeting, Edward ordered Commander Thomas to open the complaint box.

There were only a few people including his companions and Commander Thomas, present in the hall.

Commander Thomas read all the letters one by one.

Commander: Your's Sincerely Rebecca Rosy...

Street -4, Greenland House.

One companion: Poor Lady, her flower shop was her only medium for earning.

King Edward: Find her brother & bring him here, wherever he is, who has taken over her flower shop.

Second Companion: Your order will be obeyed, "Your Majesty"

Commander Thomas: Shall I? "Your Majesty" King Edward: Yes Commander....

Commander: "Letter No. -10

"Our Respected King,

Pardon me for bothering you, Sir. I just want to draw your kind attention towards the person who is roaming around in our Town nowadays.

I wonder if he is an imposter. He stalks me everywhere. Be it my home or my workplace. He claims that he likes me, but I know he doesn't.

He also misguides my brother. He is cunning and dangerous. He tells everyone that he is a visitor here in our town.

He looks Tall, He attires a long trench coat with a hat. He wears black clothes most of the time. And sometimes he wears..... Mask...

Commander Thomas looked at Edward and took a pause

King Edward: Give it to me.

Commander gave a letter to the king then gestured, the hall became empty in the next second.

And Edward read further

"I am afraid he might take my brother away. I only have my brother. We two live alone in our hut. I am an older one.

Please help us. I am worried. I hate him so much. I pray you catch him soon and chastise him.

I have the honor to remain, Sir.

Your Majesty's Humble and obedient servant. Lily Margaret,

Behind the forest,

The only Hut...

Edward got silent for a while, and thinks about Lily's words "I hate him so much"

He stood up from his throne

Commander Thomas: So, What are we going to do with this Imposter "Your Majesty"?

King Edward: She misunderstood me commander.

Commander: But, how did it happen?

King Edward: It won't happen again. She will never see this imposter again.

He left the hall

78

Commander: OH...Your Majesty...

Chapter 12

A month passed, Lily was returning home with Suzan.

Suzan: I told you, Our King is Very Helpful.

Lily: I don't see him anywhere. It's been a month.

Suzan: I am so happy for you Lily.

Lily: Thank you, Suzan. What would I do without you?

Suzan: No need to be formal.

Lily: But, I was thinking, what did King do to him?

Suzan: Why are you thinking about him, Lily?

Lily: Casually.

Suzan: Maybe He arrested him.

Lily: Arrested him.

She whispered

Suzan: OH Lily, Don't think about it, Leave it.

Lily reached her home

Lily: Michael, Where are you? I have got you something.

Michael: Lily ...You are back.

Lily: Yes. And I brought you something.

Michael: What?

Lily: Here you go.

Michael: Wow. Ice cream. You are the best Lily. Thank you.

Lily: You are most welcome.

Lily: Tell me, what did you do today?

She put her basket on the table

Michael: We played marbles. And I made a wooden house in the forest.

Lily: Oh That's Nice.

Michael: It took me 10 days to make it.

Lily: I would love to see it.

Michael: I will show you tomorrow.

 Lily: Okay.

She went to the kitchen and started cutting vegetables for dinner.

Michael continued

Michael: If Edward were with us, he would be so happy to see my wooden house. Where has he gone?

Lily: Who knows, he... might be gone as you told me "he was a visitor"

Michael: But Edward told me he would stay here, forever.

Lily: But he is not here. And look your Ice Cream is melting. You must eat it before it melts down.

Michael: I love you, Lily. Thank you for the Ice Cream.

Lily came and kissed him

Lily: Love you too dear.....

Edward now started working efficiently like a responsible King. He would help others. He was kind to his Kingdom. His ties with another Kingdom became strong. He also had good relations with other Kings.

But he was not feeling happy inside of his heart. He started feeling sad, he felt like happiness came to his door but then went away somewhere.

He was missing Michael, who had become home for him. His innocent face and his talks. He was missing Lily, the love of his life.

But then he came to reality and thought as if his dream had shattered. He thought that she never loved him and even she hated him for no reason.

Two weeks later, King Edward was out of the palace for hunting. He wore a casual dress but not the one he used to wear before... A long hat, coat, and mask.

He was on his Horse. He stopped his horse in the forest and looked around.

He dismounted from the horse and placed his bow and arrow on the horse.

And started walking.

Edward didn't notice he had come near Lily's hut.

When he saw the hut, he hid behind the tree.

He stood there for a minute and kept looking at the hut.

As soon as he was about to leave, he saw three men coming out of the hut.

One of them was old, and the others were young.

Then he saw Lily come out of the hut. He saw her begging in front of the Old man.

Lily: Please... Stop ... Don't go. Do something, please. I beg you.

But they didn't listen to her

Lily: Stop. Please.

She was crying, joining her hands, but seemed like an old man was not listening to her.

She fell on her knees and was crying but he didn't listen to her, rather he went away with his companion

Subsequently, they were gone, Lily wiped her tears then went into the hut.

ॐ

Chapter 13

Edward followed those people and he stopped them at a distance from the hut in the forest

King Edward: Excuse me.

Old man: Yes.

King Edward: Why was that lady begging you?

Old Man: None of your concern. May I leave?

King Edward: Stop. May I know who you are?

Old man: I am a Doctor.

King Edward: What's the matter? Why the lady was begging you? Tell me.

Old man: Her brother is sick. He has been suffering from an abdominal infection for a long time, I was treating him.

And today she called me again, but when I asked her for money before operating the boy. She only gave me some pennies and said, she didn't have enough money at the moment. She would pay me later.

King Edward: And. what is wrong with that?

Old man: But what if she doesn't?

King Edward: She will pay you if she is saying.

Old Man: who knows? Well, we have to go now.

King Edward: Excuse me. You must operate the child. It's your duty.

Old man: No, money comes first then treatment.

King Edward: How dare you say such things? Go and treat that boy straight away. It's my order.

Old man: And who are you to give me an order?

They three laughed

King Edward: You better operate the boy, or

Old man: Or?

King Man: I will decapitate you.

He took something out from his boot, it was the Royal sheath from which he took a knife

Old man: "Your Majesty"

They three were shocked. They have not seen Edward in that casual outfit before. The old man fell at Edward's feet and joined his hands

Old man: Pardon me, my lord. I didn't recognize you.

I made a mistake. He cried

Old man: I apologize. Forgive us. Mercy.

 They got scared and begged for their lives

King Edward: Go & treat him first. I will see what

punishment will be given to you.

He yelled at them, they got scared and ran to Lily's

hut

Old man: Where is the boy? Come. You open the

briefcase.

Lily stood up from the chair after watching this

Other Doctor: There you go, Sir.

Old man: Mark here, fast.

The Third Doctor sent Lily outside and drew the

curtain. Lily sat down on the chair watching the

curtain, crying and praying for her brother.

Edward was standing behind the tree and waiting.

After an hour, the Old man came to Lily

Old man: Your brother is out of danger now.

Lily: Thank you. Thank you so much. I promise I will pay you as soon as I get my salary.

Old man: No, We don't want money. Take these medicines.

Old man: He is unconscious right now, it will take some time to heal him. Take care of him.

Old man: Let's go. He said to others

Lily: But Doctor...

He left the hut but Lily was behind him calling doctor

 Lily: Doctor. Stop...

Lily saw the Doctor, he was meeting someone behind the trees. The old man was joining his hand, he stayed there for five minutes then all three left lily was watching this standing at the door of the hut

Lily came there to see to whom this Old man was talking, when she reached behind the tree she found Edward, She got angry at him.

Lily: What do you think you are doing?

Lily: What do you think of yourself Mister? What do you want to prove? You think you can buy us. She cried and yelled at him

Edward didn't speak a single word to her.

Meanwhile, Commander Thomas arrived with Edward's horse which he found in the forest.

Lily: Commander, Oh, Sir, You have arrived at the right time. Arrest him. He is an imposter. Arrest him. Please.

Commander Thomas: I found your Horse in the forest, "Your Majesty"

 Commander came close to Edward and stood right behind him

Lily: Majesty?

 She whispered and looked at Edward

Lily felt embarrassed and stood up with her downcast eyes.

Edward didn't speak a single word and silently moved to the hut to see Michael.

Commander: May I too?

 Commander asked

King Edward: No.

The door of the hut was smaller than his height, he bent down to go through it.

There was only a fan which was hanging from the ceiling of the hut. The fan was small.

 Michael's bed was right below the fan.

Edward dragged the chair and sat down on it next to the bed. Lily was standing with her eyes down behind the tree

Commander Thomas: Your Imposter is our King.

Lily started crying to hear that

Commander Thomas: OH Stop crying "Young lady"

Lily: I am ashamed. I thought him a bad man. I insulted him. I can't count, how many times. "Sir"

Commander Thomas: I know...

Lily: I insulted Our King. OH JESUS.

 She cried

Lily: Sir Could you answer me one question?

Commander: yes please

Lily: What punishment will he give me?

Commander Thomas: Go... and ask him yourself.

Lily: I won't even be able to make an eye contact with him, let alone speak to him.

Commander Thomas: go..

Soon, Lily gathered courage and went into the hut. Edward was sitting, holding Michael's hand, Michael was still unconscious.

He let go of Michael's hand when he heard Lily's Footsteps, he stood up from the chair

King Edward: Who knows, you may not like me holding your brother's hand. Who knows, you might put a letter against me in the complaint box again. Who knows, you might insult me again.

Who knows, you might misunderstood my intentions.

Who knows, you might judge me for no reason.

King Edward: Anyway.... Take care of him.

 He was about to go

Lily: Stop. I don't know. I don't know whether I should say sorry first or... Thank you.

If you hadn't come on time, my brother... my brother...

She cried

Lily: Thank you. Thank you. I can never repay you for this favour.

Lily: And. And I want to apologize, whatever I did, I said, for all my misbehaviour. Pardon me, Your Majesty. Please.

He turned back, Lily was crying, her head was down, her hands were joined, and tears were falling down her cheeks.

Lily: I didn't know, you are Our King. I thought you Impersonator. Pardon me, Sir.

Edward didn't say anything so lily continued

Lily: I will accept whatever punishment you give me "your Majesty"

King Edward: I see... As we know you have insulted a King.

According to law, your punishment will be ... you will be whipped one hundred times.

Lily: What?

She lifted her head

King Edward: Yes.

He took steps towards her with his poker face

Lily: You must excuse me sir but this is no punishment for a woman.

 King Edward: This is a punishment...For a woman.

He continued

And for men, their heads are beheaded.

Lily: Heads Beheaded?

Lily was terrified

King Edward: Yes.

King Edward: What do you think? Do you accept your Punishment, Maiden?

She didn't answer, she was scared, and Edward came close to her.

King Edward: Answer me, Miss. Margaret.

Lily was silent and cried

King Edward: let's think about it .There's another punishment for you.

He whispered

King Edward: Do you think you could spend the rest of your life with this imposter?

He continued

King Edward: Will you marry me, Miss Lily Margaret?

Lily didn't believe, what she heard, a person whom she had insulted many times, whom she thought an imposter, still wanted to marry her instead of punishing her.

She looked at him.

King Edward: I've always been clear with my intentions. I've never felt this way before for anyone. And my feelings for you are deep and pure.

Lily said nothing but cried

King Edward: Tell me, do you accept this punishment?

He whispered

Lily looked down

Lily: Pardon me "Your Majesty" This is not a match. You are... You are the King. I am nothing but a servant. "You must marry a princess"

She would be your appropriate companion.

King Edward: But I've found my companion, my perfect match, I found my happiness in you Miss Margaret... And I don't think I can be happy with anyone but you.

Edward held her hand, as Edward held Lily's Hand she felt warmth, comfort, and connection that words could not describe.

 She looked up to see Edward's face

King Edward: I don't see any difference between us. All I see... I genuinely love you. And you also have feelings for me. And I know that too....

She was silently looking at him

Lily: Still. I can't marry you. She looked at Michael.

King Edward: But what if we share responsibilities?

Edward smiled to look towards Michael then he looked at Lily.

Lily said nothing but smiled

A month later, they got married, and everyone was happy in the palace. Commander Thomas was very happy finally Edward found his happiness.

Michael was very excited, he always wanted Edward to marry Lily.

Michael: I knew, it would happen one day Edward.

Oops ... Pardon me "Your Majesty"

 Michael bowed down

Edward bent down and came to Michael's face.

King Edward: Edward...I will always be "Edward" for you. Your friend Edward...

"A visitor"

Michael: OH Edward.... I love you.....

He hugged Edward

And they all lived happily after

&